⋆ NIXIE NESS ⋆

COOKING STAR

AFTER-SCHOOL SUPERSTARS

★ NIXIE NESS ★★

COOKING STAR

Claudia Mills

pictures by Grace Zong

MARGARET FERGUSON BOOKS

HOLIDAY HOUSE · NEW YORK

Margaret Ferguson Books

Text copyright © 2018 by Claudia Mills

Illustrations copyright © 2018 by Grace Zong

All Rights Reserved

HOLIDAY HOUSE is registered in the U.S. Patent and Trademark Office

Printed and bound in August 2020 at Maple Press, York, PA, U.S.A.

www.holidayhouse.com

First paperback edition published in 2020

1 3 5 7 9 10 8 6 4 2

Library of Congress Cataloging-in-Publication Data

Names: Mills, Claudia, author. | Zong, Grace, illustrator. Title:
Nixie Ness, cooking star / Claudia Mills ; pictures by Grace Zong.
Description: First edition. | New York : Holiday House, [2019]
Series: After-School Superstars ; [#1] | "Margaret Ferguson Books."
Summary: Nixie and Grace have been best and only friends since
preschool, but now Nixie must attend an after-school cooking camp
while Grace spends her afternoons with classmate Elyse.
Identifiers: LCCN 2018028213 | ISBN 9780823440931 (hardcover)
Subjects: | CYAC: Best friends—Fiction. | Friendship—Fiction.
Cooking—Fiction. After-school programs—Fiction. Schools—Fiction.
Classification: LCC PZ7.M63963 Nix2019 | DDC [Fic]—dc23
LC record available at https://lccn.loc.gov/2018028213

ISBN: 978-0-8234-4093-1 (hardcover)

ISBN: 978-0-8234-4603-2 (paperback)

To Wina Mortenson

★ NIXIE NESS ★★

COOKING STAR

★ one ★

"COME back, puppy noses!" Nixie Ness scolded.

She had just snipped a black jelly bean in half, to make two candy noses for two puppy-face cupcakes. And both noses had practically jumped off the kitchen counter and onto the floor.

Her best friend, Grace Kenny, burst out laughing, and Nixie laughed, too. She loved whenever she said or did something Grace thought was extra-funny. Nixie and Grace had been best friends since their first day at Sunflower Preschool, when Grace had been crying and two-year-old Nixie had taken her by the hand.

As far as Nixie was concerned, the only thing better than baking cupcakes was baking cupcakes on a Friday afternoon with your best friend in the whole world. And the only thing better than *that* was decorating them to look like puppy faces, with jelly-bean eyes and noses, and ears of pink taffy drooping down on either side of their frosted heads.

Usually Nixie's mother made Nixie and Grace eat healthy snacks after school, like celery and carrot sticks with hummus, or apple slices spread with peanut butter. But for some reason her mom had been willing to let them make a special snack today. She'd even taken them grocery shopping after school to get the ingredients.

"Let's use whole jelly beans instead," Grace suggested. "That would be easier than trying to cut them in half."

"They can be puppies with really big eyes and noses," Nixie agreed. "Like instead of cocker spaniels, they can be cocker nosels. Or instead of Welsh corgis, they can be Welsh nosies."

Grace laughed again and licked buttercream frosting from her fingers.

"You have chocolate frosting on your cheek," Nixie informed her.

Grace swiped at the wrong cheek with her chocolate-covered finger. Now she had a big dark smear across each cheek, matching the long dark hair that Nixie thought was much prettier than her own stubby blonde braids.

"Well, you have chocolate frosting all over your nose," Grace said.

Nixie went to look at herself in the glass door of the microwave. Grace followed. At the sight of their matching chocolate-covered faces, both girls burst out laughing again.

"We're the chocolate-frosting twins!" Nixie said.

Lots of the kids in their third-grade class—including Grace—had parents who worked away from home. Some of the kids stayed at Longwood Elementary for the after-school program; others took the shuttle bus to the YMCA or went to other places until their parents were ready to pick them up. Nixie felt lucky that her mother worked at home as a part-time website designer, so Grace could come to Nixie's house every afternoon.

"We still have six more cupcakes to do," Grace said, as they wiped the chocolate off their faces. "Let's make some kitten ones, okay?"

The website Nixie had found on her mother's tablet showed pictures and instructions for kitten cupcakes, too.

"The puppy ones are cuter," Nixie told her.

"I think the kitten ones are cuter," Grace replied.

Nixie stared at Grace. How could her best friend not see that the puppy cupcakes were the cutest cupcakes on planet Earth?

But just yesterday Grace had said that if her parents ever let her get a pet, she had changed her mind and wanted a cat, not a dog. Even though she and Nixie had been begging their parents for a dog *forever*. They had already promised each other they'd share the dog, depending on which set of parents relented first. Nixie had zero interest in sharing a cat.

"Do you know what Elyse said yesterday when we were lining up for library time?" Grace continued. "She's getting a *kitten*. This weekend. From the Humane Society. A kitten of her very *own*. To *keep*."

Nixie gave a shrug. Elyse Sandia was in

their class at school, and if she was getting a puppy, Nixie would have tried to think of yet another scheme to make her parents let her get one. But Elyse could have a hundred thousand kittens and Nixie wouldn't mind a bit.

"Well, you can make three kitten cupcakes," Nixie finally said, "and I'll make three more puppy ones." It was silly to fuss over how to decorate the cupcakes on their special baking day.

"You know what I was thinking?" Grace asked.

"What?" Nixie had already picked up a spoonful of brown frosting to start in on her three puppy faces.

"We could invite Elyse to come over to your house with us after school sometime. Her dad works at home, like your mom does, so she doesn't go to any after-school program, either."

Nixie stared at Grace again, longer and harder this time. Occasionally, as a favor for somebody's mom, another classmate came to Nixie's house after school, but those days were never Nixie's favorites. Why would Grace spoil their best-friend fun on purpose? But before she could think of what to say in reply, her mother came into the kitchen.

"Oh, those are adorable, girls!" Nixie's mother pulled out her phone to snap some pictures of the girls standing next to the two cupcakes that looked most puppylike. Nixie and Grace made normal smiles for the first photo and then hung out their tongues and held up begging puppy paws for the others until they both dissolved in a fit of giggles.

As Nixie's mom returned the phone to the pocket of her jeans, her mouth twitched the way it always did when she was about to say something she wasn't sure Nixie was going to like.

"Why don't you take a little decorating break," she said. "I have some news. It affects both of you, so Grace's mother said it was all right if I told you together."

Nixie's chest tightened as she and Grace plopped down into chairs at the kitchen table.

"You know how I've been talking about finding a new job?"

Nixie relaxed. Her mother had been talking about getting a go-off-to-work job ever since Nixie started kindergarten. First she was planning to look for a job at the public library because she loved books so much. Then she was going to apply for a job at Nixie's school because she loved kids so much. Nothing ever happened.

"Well, I heard this morning that I got the job I applied for back in August," her mother said. "They want me to start right away, on Monday."

Nixie and Grace exchanged stunned glances.

"What kind of job?" Grace asked.

"A wonderful job. Working in a bookstore. And not just any bookstore. The new children's bookstore downtown."

It did sound like the perfect job for a person who loved books *and* kids. Her mother looked so happy that Nixie wanted to be happy for her, too. But if this was really such a terrific thing, why had her mother's mouth been so twitchy? And what was going to happen after school?

Nixie could hear her voice coming out squeaky. "Will you work all day? Will Grace and I go to the after-school program?"

She'd bet anything there would be no baking of puppy *or* kitten cupcakes there. And the after-school teachers, like every grown-up they'd ever known, would tell her and Grace that it wasn't nice to play by themselves so much. They'd talk on and on about "including others." Nixie didn't want to include others, unless the other was a dog.

"The after-school program is tons of fun," Grace offered, her face brightening. "It really truly is."

"Says who?" Nixie asked.

"Says everybody," Grace replied.

Nixie had heard over morning announcements that Longwood Elementary School had a new program this year called After-School Superstars, with a different "camp" for each grade each month. But she had barely listened to the details, knowing that she and Grace would never have to go to it.

Grace kept on talking. "I forget what the

first camp was, the one we already missed, but the next camp for our grade is—ta-da!—a cooking camp! I think we'll like it, Nixie."

This was vastly worse than Grace saying she thought kitten cupcakes were cuter than puppy cupcakes or wanting to invite Elyse over to play.

"Actually . . . ," Nixie's mom said slowly.

"Actually, what?" Nixie tried to keep her voice from wobbling.

Her mother hesitated before replying.

"Nixie, *you're* going to attend the after-school program. Grace's mother is making other plans."

Nixie remembered that the reason Grace had started spending afternoons at Nixie's house in the first place was because the after-school programs cost too much.

Nixie reached over for Grace's hand the same way she had done on the first day of pre-school.

Grace squeezed her hand tight.

They decorated the last six cupcakes in silence. Nixie no longer cared that Grace was putting kitten whiskers made of strands of black licorice on hers. What did anything matter if they'd never be together at Nixie's house after school, just the two of them, ever again?

When Grace's father picked Nixie up for a ride to their soccer game on Saturday morning, Nixie leaned across the backseat to hug Grace as if they had been apart for a month instead of a night.

"I wish you were coming to cooking camp, too," Nixie whispered. How could Nixie go to an after-school program without her best friend by her side? And what would Grace do after school every day without her? "Did your mom figure out what you're doing instead?"

Grace gave her a reassuring smile. "It's going to be okay. She found another friend's house for me to go to every day."

"Which friend?" Nixie asked.

"My mom called Elyse's mom—they've been coming to our church—and I'm going there."

To *Elyse's* house? With Elyse and her *kitten*?

Grace must have seen the tears welling in

Nixie's eyes. "I know," she said. "I wish I was going to the after-school program with you, Nixie. I really do."

Nixie knew Grace meant it. But right now Grace didn't seem to be as close to tears as Nixie was.

Having a new job was great for Nixie's mom.

Playing with someone else's kitten was apparently okay for Grace.

So the only person this was completely, totally, absolutely terrible for was Nixie.

★ two ★

ON Monday morning Nixie gave her house a long, lingering glance of farewell. She wouldn't see it again until after one of her parents picked her up from cooking camp at five thirty.

She did her best to act normal at school. She and Grace whispered together during math until Mrs. Townsend had to shush them. They giggled together during P.E., which started off with some yoga stretches including one called Salute to the Sun. Nixie always said, "Hi, sun!" and Grace always laughed when she did. They ate lunch together, as they did every day, without any mention of cooking camp, or Elyse's new kitten, or how they'd never have after-school time together again as long as they lived.

At three o'clock the closing bell rang.

Grace gave Nixie a good-bye hug. "Don't have too much fun without me!" she whispered.

"I won't!" Nixie whispered back.

She pretended not to see the smile Grace gave Elyse as the two of them headed out of the classroom together.

Nixie shouldered her backpack and lined up to trudge off with the other after-school kids from Mrs. Townsend's third-grade classroom. The cooking camp was meeting in the cafeteria. The little kids, who weren't old enough for the special camps yet, were having their after-school program in the gym; other camps, Nixie had heard in the morning announcements, were meeting in the library, the music room, and the art room.

Vera Vance, a new girl in Nixie's class this year, fell into place behind her at the classroom door.

"*You're* going to cooking camp?" Vera asked. "I thought you always went home after school with Grace."

Nixie thought of a remark she had heard her father say once. "That was then. This is now," she told Vera.

She liked *then* better.

In line ahead of her she saw Nolan Nanda, the smartest boy in Mrs. Townsend's class. Nolan was a know-it-all, but not a braggy know-it-all, in Nixie's opinion. He just happened to be a walking library of all kinds of facts (usually weird facts) about all kinds of things (usually weird things). A lot of other kids thought *he* was weird. But weird wasn't necessarily a bad thing to be.

In front of Nolan, Boogie Bass was bouncing up and down as if that would start the line moving forward. "I heard we're going to make pizza!" he called out to anyone who might be listening. "I heard we're going to make homemade ice cream!"

If they did make pizza, Nixie thought, it would probably taste like cardboard with ketchup spread on top. If they did make ice cream, hers would probably fall off its cone and splat onto the floor.

Was Grace at Elyse's house yet? Or were they still riding in Elyse's father's car? Parents should have to ask their kids first before getting jobs that changed everything!

The head camp lady, named Colleen, checked off each camper as they filed into the cafeteria, stashed their backpacks in a corner, and sat down in the middle of the bare, hard linoleum floor. The lunchtime tables were all put away, except for four covered with what must be cooking stuff, set up in a row right next to the kitchen.

When it was Nixie's turn, Colleen said, "Welcome to After-School Superstars!" as she made a mark by Nixie's name on her attendance sheet. "I'm sure you'll have lots of friends here from your grade."

Nixie didn't bother to tell Colleen that the only friend she wanted to be with was Grace.

Once all the campers had been checked in, Colleen introduced the cooking camp instructors, Chef Michael and Chef Maggie, who ran cooking classes for kids all over the city, and even for grown-ups who wanted to learn how to cook extra-fancy foods.

"Welcome, future chefs!" Chef Maggie greeted them.

"Be prepared to eat some of the best food of your lives, cooked by you!" Chef Michael exclaimed.

Nixie gazed down at her shoes as Chef Michael and Chef Maggie kept on talking, talking, talking. She forced herself to listen as Chef Maggie explained the amazing things they would be doing together over the next four weeks.

Learning how to make their own healthy lunches. Who cared?

Being filmed for a new episode of Chef Michael and Chef Maggie's online video series, *Kids Can Cook*. Parents had already signed the permission slips. All right, that sounded like fun. Or it would have been fun if Grace and Nixie were going to be in the video together.

Holding a huge bake sale to raise money for a charity the campers would get to vote on. Exploring cuisines from around the world: Italy, Mexico, West Africa, India. Those could both be fun, too. Maybe.

Even making dog and cat treats. But what if your parents wouldn't let you have a dog?

Chef Michael started talking about something called pita pockets. That was what they were going to be making today, as an easy, get-to-know-one-another project. The teams would prepare fillings to stuff into round, flat half circles of bread with a slit in the middle. The slit turned the pita bread into a kind of pocket.

Chef Maggie told them they could pick their own four-person groups. Nixie peered around to find anyone else who looked lost and lonely, preferably three lost and lonely people who could form one lost and lonely group together.

Vera was by herself. Should Nixie go over and stand next to her? Nolan and Boogie had already teamed up. They seemed as opposite as two people could be, but they often hung out together. "Opposites attract" was another of her father's sayings. But Nixie and Grace hadn't been opposites. They had been exactly the same in every way—except for Grace's new fondness for cats.

Nolan and Boogie waved Vera over to join them.

Go ask if you can be in their group, too!
Nixie commanded herself. But she remained
stuck in place.

Then Vera approached Nixie and said, in a
super-polite way, as if she was reciting a mem-
orized line from a book on good manners for
kids, "Would you like to be in our group?"

"Sure," Nixie said, relieved. "I mean,
thanks."

Before they could start cooking anything,
they had to put on chef aprons and wash their
hands in the kitchen's three enormous sinks,
supervised by both chefs and Colleen. With sixteen campers, it took so long that Nixie thought
the camp should be renamed Hand-Washing
Camp. Ha! Let parents try convincing their
kids to sign up for *that*.

Back in the cafeteria, the four teams were
each assigned a station at one of the four tables. Standing behind the kitchen counter that
opened onto the cafeteria, Chef Maggie showed
the campers the kid-safe knives they would be
using to chop the filling ingredients into little
pieces: carrots, celery, apples, and something

dark green with frilly edges called kale. Fortunately, whatever needed to be washed had been washed ahead of time, or else the whole camp would have been spent doing nothing but standing at the sinks washing, washing, washing.

Chef Michael gave a long demonstration about peeling and chopping techniques, but it was hard for Nixie to make herself listen to every single word.

"All right, teams," he finally said. "Have at it!"

He stopped by Nixie's team for a minute or two to watch them start peeling their carrots before going off to check on another team at another table. Peeling looked so easy when Chef Michael did it, but it turned out to be surprisingly hard to peel the skin off carrots without also peeling the skin off fingers.

At last it was time for chopping. Nixie was in charge of celery. Trying not to think about Grace and Elyse, she concentrated on her task as if she were a celery-chopping machine. *Chop. Chop. Chop.*

Vera leaned over to look at Nixie's celery pieces. "Are yours too big? Or are my apple ones too small?"

Nixie paused to compare her celery pieces to Vera's apple pieces. Hers were bigger, but so what? Was there a law that every single item put into a pita pocket had to be exactly the same size?

"They look fine to me," Nixie said.

"I think Chef Michael said they should be a quarter of an inch in each direction." Vera sounded worried.

Nixie couldn't believe anyone would care so much about the size of celery pieces that were just going to be stuffed into a pita pocket where nobody would see them anyway.

She checked out the chopping of her other two teammates.

Boogie was chopping too fast. Already the floor beneath the table was thick with flying carrot bits.

Nolan hardly glanced at his heap of kale as he chopped. He was too busy explaining the origin of pita bread in some place named

Mesopotamia four thousand years ago. Had he known they were going to be making pita pockets today, or did he just happen to have a bunch of pita bread facts crammed into his head?

"I'm going to start making my apple pieces a tiny bit bigger," Vera said. "And maybe you should make your celery pieces a tiny bit smaller? Then they'll both be the same size."

Nixie had no intention of being pita-pocket twins with Vera.

"Look at Boogie's carrot pieces," she said, as Boogie stooped down to retrieve a whole carrot that had somehow landed on the floor. "Some of them are teensy-weensy, and some are humongous."

"I know," Vera said, lowering her voice. "But the thing is . . . Well, Boogie . . ."

Nixie knew Vera didn't want to come right out and say that Boogie was a terrible carrot-cutter-upper.

"I read somewhere that pita bread is the oldest bread in the world," Nolan was explaining. "That's pretty cool, don't you think? Right now, we're standing here cutting up fillings to stuff into the oldest kind of bread on earth. And guess what—*ow*!"

A piece of Boogie's carrot hit Nolan squarely in the forehead.

"Are you okay?" Boogie asked, red-faced.

Nolan gave Boogie a comforting grin as he rubbed his forehead.

"What's the deal with carrot pieces?" Boogie asked mournfully. "Why do they fly around so much more than celery or apple pieces?"

"I think," Nolan said, in his usual serious, scientific-sounding way, "it's not the fault of the *carrots*."

Nixie looked over at Vera and almost burst into giggles. But in the nick of time she caught herself. Nixie didn't want to laugh at anything if Grace wasn't there laughing with her.

"Time to finish up your chopping!" Chef Michael called.

Nixie laid down her knife as Chef Maggie started showing the teams how to mix chickpeas—whatever chickpeas were—with lemon juice squeezed from real lemons. She wondered if Vera would freak out about exactly how much lemon juice to put on the chickpeas, and if Nolan knew as many facts about chickpeas as he did about pita bread, and if Boogie would manage to avoid injuring any of his teammates with flying chickpeas.

But mostly she wondered what Grace and Elyse were doing right now.

★ three ★

AT lunch on Thursday, Nixie chomped down hard on her cashew-butter sandwich and chewed with all her might.

"I tried and I tried, but I couldn't think of the right name for him," Elyse was saying. "At first I thought Button. Because he has this little white spot in the middle of his tummy."

"Besides," Grace said to Nixie, "you know that expression 'cute as a button'?"

Nixie took a big swallow of sandwich, but it stuck in her throat. Grace had never asked Nixie, *Do you mind if Elyse eats with us?* She hadn't said, *I'm sorry, but she really wants to, and I can't get out of it without hurting her feelings.* Instead, Elyse had showed up at their cafeteria table on Tuesday and had now sat with them at lunch for three whole days. During P.E.

that morning, Elyse had placed herself right between Nixie and Grace, and when Nixie had said, "Hi, sun!" Elyse had said, "Hi, sun!" too, and Grace had laughed equally hard for both of them.

"But I don't know, Button didn't seem to fit," Elyse went on. "Then yesterday we came up with the absolutely perfect name!"

Grace took up the story. "We were doing this dance called the cha-cha."

So now Grace and Elyse were *dancing* together?

"It goes like this," Grace continued. "One, two, cha-cha-cha." She stood up to demonstrate: one step forward, one step back, three quick steps in place.

"And my kitten kept getting in the way of our feet," Elyse interrupted. "So it was more like one, two, cha-cha-crash!"

"And then I said, that's it, that's his name!" Grace finished.

"His name is Crash?" Nixie asked, trying to have something to contribute to the conversation. At lunch on Tuesday and Wednesday, Grace had asked her a whole bunch of

questions about what cooking camp was like, but Nixie hadn't felt like talking about it when Elyse was right there listening, so she had hardly said anything. Now all they talked about was cats, cats, cats.

"No!" both Grace and Elyse said together. "It's Cha-Cha!"

This might have been the dumbest name for a cat Nixie had ever heard. But Grace and Elyse were both laughing so hard at its funniness and wonderfulness they didn't even notice Nixie wasn't laughing with them.

Then and there Nixie decided: she needed to make a Plan.

A Plan to get her best friend back soon—like *now*—or lose her forever.

The only problem was that she had no idea what the Plan could be.

☆ ☆ ☆

At cooking camp that afternoon, they were baking healthy muffins to put in a healthy lunch. On Monday they had assembled the healthy pita pockets. On Tuesday they had put together healthy yogurt parfaits (nonfat, low-sugar vanilla yogurt layered with blueberries and raspberries, and homemade granola) and healthy fruit kebabs (alternating grapes and melon balls stuck on extra-long toothpicks). On Wednesday they had made healthy pasta salad with whole-grain pasta that looked like little bow ties, lots and lots of veggies, and chopped-up hard-boiled eggs. Nixie had to admit everything had been surprisingly tasty.

Now they were baking healthy Morning Glory muffins, which had nothing to do with morning glories, which Nixie knew were blue flowers that climbed up a trellis in her front yard in the summer. The Morning Glory muffins were healthy because they were made with whole-wheat instead of white flour and honey and orange juice instead of sugar, and had grated carrots and apples, walnut pieces, sunflower seeds, shredded coconut, and raisins added into them, too.

"Why are they called Morning Glory muffins?" Nixie asked Nolan, after Chef Michael and Chef Maggie had finished their demonstration and the teams were busy at their stations.

"Because people eat muffins for breakfast in the *morning*?" Nolan suggested. "And because these muffins are so nutritious and delicious that they're *glorious*?"

That made sense. Everything Nolan said made sense.

"But we're supposed to put them in healthy *lunches*," Vera pointed out. "So when we eat them it won't be morning anymore." Nixie had visions of Vera at home checking her clock to make sure it wasn't too late in the day to eat a morning-only muffin.

"I want to be eating them right now!" Boogie chimed in.

Nixie started reading out the list of dry ingredients while Vera did the measuring. The good thing about Vera doing the measuring was that you knew every single ingredient would be measured perfectly. The bad thing was that it took Vera forever to do it.

"Two cups of whole-wheat flour," Nixie read.

Vera transferred flour into the measuring cup, one slow spoonful at a time, until it was full to the very top. With the side of a butter knife, she leveled off the flour so there wasn't a single speck extra and carefully poured it into the mixing bowl. Then she began measuring the second cup with the same precision.

Boogie was working on the wet ingredients—honey, vegetable oil, orange juice, vanilla, and three eggs—while Nolan was busy peeling and grating the carrots and apples. Maybe Boogie should have been the one peeling and grating, and Nolan should have been the one breaking the eggs. But Boogie already had the first egg in his hand.

Crack!

The eggshell shattered on the side of the stainless-steel mixing bowl. Part of the egg fell into the bowl. Most of the egg splattered onto the table.

Vera looked up from leveling off her first teaspoon of baking soda, eyes wide with horror. Nixie stifled a giggle.

"I can scoop up the rest of it," Boogie promised cheerfully.

The egg, dripping off the side of the table now, was plainly beyond scooping.

"That's okay," he said. "I'll get another egg from Chef Maggie!"

Boogie was already darting into the kitchen.

And then he was on his way back, waving the egg in the air as if it were a toy flag at a Fourth of July parade, when he dropped it, sending it smashing onto the linoleum floor.

Chef Maggie brought over the next egg and supervised the breaking. Finished with all the grating, Nolan took over some of Vera's measuring. He was not only their team's best grater, but as a measurer, he was accurate *and* fast. Once they had stirred all the ingredients together in the big mixing bowl, and the batter had been spooned into the muffin tins, the muffins from all the teams went into the kitchen's huge double oven to bake for twenty minutes. Colleen told the campers they could either use the break to get a start on homework or head outside for a game of tag.

Nixie didn't see a single person choosing to do homework except for Vera who probably needed extra time to check each math problem five times to make sure every answer was perfect. But Nixie didn't feel like playing tag, either. She hated tag, where she always ended up as "it," with everyone else screaming as they ran away from her. If only she could be baking

Morning Glory muffins at home with Grace. Or even having Grace baking them with her here at camp. Grace would have thought Boogie's egg calamity was hilarious, too.

Instead Grace was at Elyse's doing the cha-cha with a cat.

Nolan must not have liked tag, either, because he joined Nixie outside in the shade by the brick wall of the school. Boogie, who had chosen to be "it," yelled cheerfully as he dashed around in unsuccessful pursuit of everyone else.

"I'm going to surprise my sisters by making some healthy lunches for them next week, using our recipes," Nolan told Nixie. "They're both stressed about middle-school cheerleading tryouts, so I thought I'd give them a treat."

"Wow," Nixie said. She didn't even make her own lunches, let alone make lunches as a surprise for anyone else.

Just like that, the perfect Get Your Best Friend Back Plan popped into Nixie's head. Yes! She'd make one big, ultra-surprising, mega-amazing lunch for Grace, with *all* the healthy things that they had made in it, the best lunch that anyone had ever made for anyone else in the history of the world.

Grace would say, *I can't believe you went to so much trouble to make such a delicious and nutritious lunch for me!*

Oh, it was nothing, Nixie would say. *It's just, you know, what best friends do for each other.*

Then Grace would remember she was best friends with Nixie, not with Elyse. Even if Elyse brought an even better lunch for Grace next week—not that Elyse *could* make a better lunch because Elyse didn't go to cooking camp—it would be clear Elyse was copying Nixie. Who would want to be best friends with a copycat?

How lucky Nixie was that the first after-school camp had been cooking and not robotics! Instead of making a special lunch to win Grace back, she would have had to build Grace her own personal robot. Nixie giggled at the thought of smuggling a robot to school in her backpack.

She gave Nolan a radiant smile and kept on smiling as the campers headed inside.

Five minutes later she tasted the first bite of a warm, soft, sweet, totally luscious Morning Glory muffin.

By this time tomorrow Nixie would have her best friend back again.

★ four ★

"**O**H, Nixie," her mother said, when Nixie explained the Plan to her parents at dinner that night. She didn't tell them it was a Get Your Best Friend Back Plan. She just said she wanted to make a special lunch for Grace tomorrow the way Nolan was making special lunches for his sisters. "We've had such a long day. I don't think I can face going grocery shopping."

"But I already have the muffins," Nixie said. Each camper had gotten a bag of muffins to take home. "So I only have to make the pita pockets, and the yogurt parfaits, and the fruit kebabs. Oh, and the pasta salad."

"Those are the *only* things you have to make?" her father asked in a teasing voice.

Nixie ignored him and turned her pleading gaze on her mother, who usually gave in faster than her father did. She tried to pretend she was an irresistibly cute puppy dog with huge, brown, sad-sad eyes, begging for a puppy treat.

Please, please, please, please, PLEASE!

"Oh, all right," her mother finally said. "We'd better go now before I collapse in an exhausted little heap."

As her mother was getting her purse, Nixie overheard her saying to her father, "I'm just glad it sounds like she's enjoying the camp activities. This is a big adjustment for her." And she overheard her father saying, "I know."

Nixie remembered to grab the sheaf of photocopied recipes chefs Maggie and Michael had sent home, so she'd have the lists of the ingredients she needed. She and Grace hardly ever talked on the phone, but as soon as she got back, she'd call Grace and tell her, *Don't bring a lunch tomorrow! Because I have a tremendous, stupendous, fabuloso surprise!* And Grace would say, *What is it?* And Nixie would say, *If I told you, it wouldn't be a surprise*, and Grace would laugh the way Nixie loved best.

It would have been more fun preparing the huge healthy lunch if Vera, Nolan, and Boogie had been there to help. Of course, it would have been the most fun if Grace had been Nixie's lunch-making partner, the two of them working together. But then Nixie wouldn't have needed the Plan in the first place.

Nixie was more grateful than ever that she already had the muffins. Her mother had vetoed the pasta salad: "You'll have plenty without it." But there was still lots of tedious, lonely peeling and chopping to do by herself.

The next morning her mother helped her pack the lunch in two matching insulated lunch bags she had found at a yard sale. Patterned with purple pansies edged with purple piping, the bags looked adorable sitting on the kitchen counter side by side. Nixie tingled with anticipation, as if she had swallowed a huge gulp of soda that was now fizzing deep inside her.

She kept the lunches hidden in her backpack so Grace wouldn't see them until the big moment. Then at lunchtime she told Grace to go ahead to the cafeteria while she retrieved the lunches from her cubby.

As she entered the cafeteria, Grace waved to her from their favorite table by the window.

Elyse waved at her, too.

The fizzy bubbles in Nixie's stomach felt a little less fizzy and bubbly.

As Nixie had instructed, Grace had no lunch box on the table in front of her.

Neither did Elyse.

Maybe Elyse was going to buy the school lunch. Lots of kids did, especially on pizza day.

But then why wasn't Elyse standing in line with the other pizza buyers?

Slowly Nixie approached the table, clutching a purple-pansy-patterned bag in each hand.

"Ooh!" Grace said, as Nixie set the matching bags on the table. They looked even more darling there than they had at home.

"Are those for *us*?" Elyse asked.

No! They're not for you! One is for Grace, and one is for me! Because we're *the best friends, and* you're *the best-friend stealer!*

But Nixie couldn't make herself say that.

She just couldn't.

"I was going to buy pizza," Elyse continued,

"but Grace told me you had a surprise for us, and we weren't supposed to eat anything first."

Nixie's fizz had fizzled out completely. Grace obviously thought Nixie was nice enough that she wouldn't bring a surprise treat for one friend and not the other. But how could you be *best* friends with more than one person?

"Yes!" Nixie said brightly. "These are special lunches! I made them!" Then she added a feeble "Ta-da!"

"But where's yours?" Grace asked.

It was an excellent question for which Nixie had no excellent answer.

"I made them for you and Elyse," she said, hoping she hadn't hesitated too long before replying. "Because you don't get to go to cooking camp like I do."

It came out sounding braggier than Nixie meant it to. But she might as well brag about something, given that Grace and Elyse had been bragging nonstop about Elyse's kitten and the fun the two of them were having without her. Well, she was having fun without them, too!

Except that she wasn't. Not really. Nothing

could really be fun if Grace wasn't there to share the fun with her.

"So are you getting pizza?" Elyse opened the lunch bag closest to her and started exploring the treats, which looked extra-delicious to Nixie right now.

"Sure!" Nixie said.

Her parents had paid ahead for a bunch of lunches, so there was money on her account.

"Umm! This is sooooo good!" Elyse said, gulping down a huge spoonful of the yogurt parfait that should have been Nixie's.

"Muffins!" Grace squealed, as she took the first bite of hers.

"Morning Glory muffins," Nixie corrected her.

Glorious Morning Glory muffins.

She could still hear Grace and Elyse squealing over the adorableness of the fruit kebabs as she trudged over to get her tray, onto which the lunchroom lady would dump one piece of limp, saggy, greasy, un-glorious pizza.

☆ ☆ ☆

Nixie and Grace had their third soccer game of the season on Saturday morning. Thank

goodness Elyse did gymnastics instead. Nixie's dad took both girls out for lunch afterward while her mom was at the bookstore. Her mom's hours varied a lot at the store: most weekday afternoons, but some Saturdays and Sundays, too, as those were the store's especially popular shopping times. But even on the occasional school-day afternoons when her mom was still home, her parents had said they didn't want Nixie to "miss out on the full camp experience." But what about missing out on the full best-friend experience?

While they waited for their burgers, Grace made Nixie feel better about the ball Nixie had kicked out of bounds, and Nixie told Grace how unfair the ref had been to call two fouls on Grace.

"I love soccer," Grace said. "Even when we lose."

"Me too!"

"I'm trying to talk Elyse into switching to soccer once her gymnastics class ends, and I think she's going to!"

Nixie knew she was supposed to say: *That's great!* But she couldn't make the words come out of her mouth. Luckily at that moment their burgers and fries arrived at the table.

Clearly, given the failure of her first attempt, Nixie needed a New and Improved Plan.

If only she could invite Grace over for something extra-super-duper special, like a sleepover. But every time she had asked in the past, Grace's mother had said no. She didn't believe in sleepovers. She claimed they should be called stay-awake-overs.

Nixie was almost relieved when lunch was done.

★ five ★

"**W**HO has a pet?" Chef Maggie asked on Monday afternoon, once Colleen had taken attendance and sixteen campers had washed up at the sinks.

At every station hands shot up into the air, frantically waving as if to say, *Call on me! Let me tell you about my pet and how amazing she is!*

Nixie's hand did not go up.

Neither did Vera's.

The two girls exchanged a small, sad smile.

Nixie already knew Boogie had a pet. She had seen him one day last summer walking a dog as big as he was, huge enough to ride like a pony. But she was surprised when Nolan raised his hand to be counted as a pet owner. He didn't seem the type to have a pet.

"What kind of pet do you have?" she asked him.

"An iguana."

Okay, that made sense.

"Campers!" Chef Maggie called over the din of kids comparing notes on their pets. "Settle down! We're going to be making pet treats today—dog biscuits and cat cookies that are a delectable and nutritious way to reward your pet for good behavior and to supplement a healthy pet diet."

"What if you don't have a pet?" someone asked. Nixie waited to hear the answer.

"Then you can give the treats to a friend who does," Chef Maggie suggested.

Ha! As if Nixie was going to give cat treats to Grace to give to Elyse to give to Cha-Cha! Cha-Cha wasn't going to get any cat treats made by Nixie—never ever. Luckily Boogie's dog could probably eat all the cat and dog treats made by all the campers and still be hungry.

Nixie didn't really listen as Chef Maggie explained how to make dog and cat treats. Luckily, Vera listened extra-hard to anything any teacher said, and Nolan usually knew everything they were going to say already. But

Nixie did collect the team's cookie cutters: bone-shaped for the dog biscuits, fish-shaped for the cat cookies.

"Why do you have an iguana?" Nixie asked Nolan as he began measuring out two cups of whole-wheat flour for the dog biscuits. "Did your parents say you couldn't have a dog?"

"I like iguanas," Nolan said. "Besides, dogs slobber."

"What about cats?" Nixie hoped he'd have something bad to say about cats, too.

"Cats scratch."

Nixie wondered if Cha-Cha had ever scratched Grace or Elyse. If he had, they certainly hadn't mentioned it.

"Why don't you have a pet?" Nixie asked Vera.

Vera didn't answer until she finished measuring exactly one tablespoon of bacon bits. As if dogs would be so fussy about having every single flavoring in their biscuits exactly right.

"My mother doesn't like pets," Vera replied.

"Any pets?"

"Any pets. She thinks they're ridiculous."

Nixie's parents didn't think pets were

ridiculous. They thought pets were too much work. And expensive.

To make the dog biscuits tasty to dogs, the whole-wheat flour was mixed with bouillon, a little cube of chicken-soup flavoring dissolved in hot water. When all the ingredients—flour, salt, vegetable oil, egg (Vera cracked open the egg this time), bouillon water, and extra treats (bacon bits)—were mixed together, the dough was kneaded into a ball. The kneading was the best part: grabbing at the dough with floury hands and giving it lots of squeezes. When the dough became a lopsided ball, the campers rolled it out, then cut it into bone shapes with the cookie cutters.

The cat cookies had tuna mixed into the dough, which was utterly unappealing in Nixie's opinion. She didn't mind eating tuna herself, but the thought of tuna cookies made her feel like gagging.

While the dog biscuits and cat cookies were baking, Chef Michael showed the campers how to make a treat for wild birds: something disgusting called suet.

To make the suet they measured two cups

of vegetable shortening—white, slippery, shiny fat that came in a can—and heated it in a pan on the stove. There were two enormous stoves in the school kitchen, but with sixteen campers, the space was crowded enough that the teams took turns, two teams in the kitchen at a time.

Once the shortening was melted, they poured it into a bowl and took it back to their table. There they added cornmeal, flour, and whatever extra treats they thought birds might like. Chef Michael and Chef Maggie had provided sunflower seeds, chopped nuts, and bits of dried fruit. The final step was to shape the mixture into patties and wrap them up in tinfoil.

"It looks gross!" Nixie moaned as she gazed down at her suet-sticky hands.

"I'm glad I'm not a bird," Vera agreed. She said it so seriously, as if she had narrowly escaped being a bird, that Nixie giggled. She could totally relate. After making those tuna-fish cookies, Nixie had been glad she wasn't a cat.

"It's all ingredients that *people* eat," Nolan pointed out.

"Vegetable shortening?" Nixie said. "People don't eat that!"

"Of course they do," Nolan said. "Not straight out of the can, but mixed in with other stuff to make piecrust, and pastries, and all kinds of things. You've just never cooked anything with it yourself before."

That was the strange thing about cooking: seeing exactly what everything you ate was made out of.

"It tastes okay," Boogie reported, taking his finger from his mouth.

"Boogie!" Nixie and Vera shrieked together.

"You stuck your *finger* in that?" Vera accused him.

"And then you *licked* it?" Nixie demanded.

"I wanted to see what it tasted like," Boogie said. Then he cheeped like a bird, for good measure.

When the dog biscuits and cat cookies came out of the oven, and the suet patties had cooled and hardened in the huge refrigerator,

it was time to divide up the treats to take home.

"I don't want any dog biscuits or cat cookies," Nixie said. Not that she wanted any suet, either.

"Chef Maggie said we could give them away to friends with dogs or cats," Vera reminded her.

"I don't have any friends with dogs or cats," Nixie said.

Vera stared at her. "Are you kidding? What about Elyse? She has that new kitten! Cha-Cha would adore fish-shaped cookies!"

Elyse isn't my friend, she's Grace's friend, Nixie wanted to say. But she had a feeling Vera would stare at her even more if she said that.

One thing Nixie knew for sure: giving cat cookies to Elyse wasn't going to help her get Grace back. Elyse and Grace would have even more fun together feeding the cookies to Cha-Cha.

"Boogie can take mine," Nixie said. She shoved her dog biscuits, cat cookies, and suet patties toward Boogie.

To her horror, Boogie grabbed one of the

dog biscuits, broke it in half, and popped a piece into his mouth.

"Boogie!" Nixie and Vera shrieked again.

Boogie gave a sharp chorus of barks. Then, tossing a cat cookie into his already-full mouth, he meowed.

"Boogie!"

But now both girls were laughing, and Nolan joined in, too.

THE rest of the week was Pumpkin Week at camp. On Tuesday afternoon, a huge pile of pumpkins appeared in a corner of the cafeteria floor, as if the camp was being held in a pumpkin patch.

"Pumpkin soup!" Chef Maggie said. "Pumpkin pancakes! And of course, pumpkin pie!"

Nixie liked pumpkin okay. Thanksgiving wouldn't be Thanksgiving without pumpkin pie. But she would turn into a pumpkin if she ate nothing but pumpkin four days in a row.

"And," Chef Maggie added, "we'll be videoing your camp for the pumpkin episode of our *Kids Can Cook* online series. Campers, this is Clove, our videographer wizard." She pointed to a young woman with spiky hair dyed in bands of bright pink, deep purple, and neon green.

"Your job, campers," Chef Maggie told them, "is to go about your work as you usually do and leave the filming up to Clove. We're not following any scripts here. We want you to be yourselves."

"Are we going to be famous?" Boogie shouted, bouncing on his heels as if he was about to bound up onstage to collect his Academy Award for Best Actor in a cooking video.

"Well," Chef Maggie said cautiously, "this is going to be a professionally produced video and we can't guarantee that every single camper will end up being featured in the final version. Clove will make the ultimate decision of what to keep and what to cut when she edits several hours of footage into a five-minute piece about our Pumpkin Week."

But surely if Clove picked any team, she'd pick Nixie's. No one else at camp was smarter than Nolan, funnier than Boogie, or more perfect than Vera. And no else at camp wanted this more than Nixie. No one else at camp *needed* it more than Nixie.

This would be the New and Improved Get Your Best Friend Back Plan! If Nixie's team was the star of the cooking video, and if the video went viral on the Internet, and if a million people saw it, or even half a million, she would be famous. Maybe she would move to Hollywood and star in real movies, and have a huge mansion with a pool and ten dogs, and she'd invite Grace to fly to California to visit, and pay for her plane ticket, too.

First, though, they had to cut up the pumpkins. The adults helped with the hardest part of the cutting, but the scooping and scraping came next. It was like making jack-o'-lanterns, but a lot less fun, because they had to do the icky part of dealing with the goo but not the cool part of cutting the scary faces.

Why not use canned pumpkin? It would be so much quicker and easier! But when someone else asked that, Chef Michael said it would be quickest and easiest to buy a pumpkin pie from the store. Quick and easy wasn't the *point*.

Nixie saw Clove scanning the teams of campers, trying to decide which one was wonderful enough to start filming first.

Pick us, pick us, pick us! Nixie beamed toward her. But it seemed that whenever Nixie looked Clove's way, Clove had her camera trained on somebody else's team.

Oh, well. No one was going to become a movie star by taking forever to cut and scoop out a week's worth of pumpkins and then roast the pumpkin slices on big cookie trays in the ovens. So it wouldn't be until Wednesday that any real pumpkin cooking could begin, and even then it was only going to be pumpkin soup.

Could Nixie really become famous enough to win Grace back by starring in a video on how to make pumpkin *soup*?

Well, she wouldn't know until she tried.

☆ ☆ ☆

At cooking camp the next day Nixie scrunched her eyes shut and clenched her fists tight to concentrate on beaming her *Pick us, pick us, pick us!* thoughts to Clove. This time it must have worked because Clove began slowly heading in their direction.

Nixie turned on her biggest movie-star

smile. Clove would want to feature kids who acted like cooking was the most fun they had ever had in their lives.

Unfortunately, as Clove approached, Vera was acting like cooking was the total opposite of fun. Brow furrowed, she scowled down at the cutting board with intense concentration, cutting each roasted pumpkin slice into squares exactly half an inch long and half an inch wide. Vera probably thought Clove would want to feature kids who were perfect pumpkin-cutting machines. But at the rate Vera was cutting, it would take a whole five-minute video for her to cut three tiny squares of pumpkin.

"Pumpkins originated in Central America," Nolan said, speaking more slowly, loudly, and distinctly than he usually did while imparting pointless trivia. "Did you know pumpkins are ninety percent water?"

He evidently thought Clove would want to feature kids who were walking encyclopedias of fascinating pumpkin facts. But Nixie couldn't imagine Clove would want to include a lot of random pumpkin facts in a video that was only going to be five minutes long.

Nixie wanted to hiss to Vera, *Smile!*

She wanted to hiss to Nolan, *Stop talking!*

She wanted to tell both of them to act normal, but this *was* acting normal for Vera and Nolan. Besides, if she whispered anything to them, the whispering would end up on the video, too.

Nixie was afraid even to look at what Boogie was doing, but maybe it was better to know the worst.

When she stole a peek, Boogie was measuring out the maple syrup that would sweeten the soup. Some of the syrup dribbled onto his fingers, and Boogie, being Boogie, licked them. Then, with the same fingers that had just been in his mouth, he scooped up a handful of Vera's pumpkin squares to dump into the pot of broth and spices they would carry into the kitchen for their turn at the stove.

Nixie stopped herself from giving her usual shriek of *Boogie!*

Clove followed their team into the kitchen. Nixie made sure to grab the spoon so she'd have her chance at stardom. Forcing herself to ignore her teammates, she did her best to smile brightly enough and stir vigorously enough to make up for Vera's panicked perfectionism, Nolan's irritating know-it-all-ism, and Boogie's total grossness.

As the soup started to bubble around the edges, Nixie gave the mixture such a powerful stir that a square of boiling pumpkin splashed out of the pan and onto her bare wrist.

"Ow!" she yelped. "Ow-ow-ow-ow-ow!"

"Are you okay?" Vera asked, her eyes wide with alarm.

"Run your wrist under cold water," Nolan advised. "Go do it right now."

Boogie scooped up the offending piece of pumpkin, blew on it a few times, and then popped it into his mouth.

Oh, what on earth must Clove be thinking? But when Nixie turned around to look at her, Clove and her camera had already moved back into the cafeteria.

Clutching her burned wrist, Nixie headed toward the sink to try Nolan's cold-water cure, tears of pain and disappointment stinging the insides of her eyes.

So much for thinking she could win Grace back by starring in an online video on how to cook pumpkin soup.

☆ ☆ ☆

Clove barely filmed their team during the rest of Pumpkin Week. Apparently, Nixie's team had blown their one and only chance. By Friday Nixie had decided she was never going to eat any pumpkin ever again.

And by Friday Nixie was almost ready to decide she would never eat lunch with Grace and Elyse ever again, either. Grace had been playing with Elyse and Cha-Cha every day after school for two full weeks. Nixie would have thought that by now Cha-Cha's antics would be less enthralling. But instead she had to hear about how Cha-Cha had gotten stuck in the laundry hamper, and how Cha-Cha had tumbled off the kitchen counter, and how loudly Cha-Cha purred for such a tiny kitten.

Grace and Elyse had started meowing as they saluted the sun in P.E. Nixie and Grace didn't even whisper during class anymore because Mrs. Townsend had threatened to start switching desks if people couldn't settle down and focus. With Nixie's luck, Mrs. Townsend would end up moving Grace right next to Elyse.

On Saturday Nixie and Grace barely had time to talk during the soccer game, which their team lost again. Grace's mother was the one who drove this time, and she didn't invite Nixie to go out for lunch afterward. She said they had "other plans."

Nixie had a terrible feeling the "other plans" might involve a girl named Elyse and a kitten named Cha-Cha.

Nixie needed another Plan of her own.

What she really needed was for her mother to quit her job so she'd be home after school again. Then there would be no reason for Nixie to go to After-School Superstars, and Grace would come to Nixie's house after school instead of going to Elyse's, and everything would be the way it used to be.

Unless . . . what if Grace picked Elyse's house with a kitten over Nixie's house without one? But she wouldn't. She couldn't. She'd choose Nixie's kitten-less house in a heartbeat because she'd really be choosing not Nixie's house, but Nixie.

So the Newer and Even More Improved Plan was to make her mother want to quit her job, to make her mother *have to* quit.

And suddenly Nixie had a brilliant idea for how to make that happen.

☆ ☆ ☆

On Sunday afternoon Nixie's father took her to visit her mother at the bookstore. The store was in an old house, on a shady street, with a staircase up to a reading loft, each step painted a different pastel hue. Her mother bustled about helping one kid find a book on how to knit and another find a book on how to do yo-yo tricks.

Did the store sell any books on how to win your best friend back? If only there was some book that would tell Nixie how to make Grace like her better than Elyse, better than anyone else, always and forever. Maybe she could ask her book-expert mom to help her find one.

At least she had her new Plan, her best Plan yet. But it gave Nixie a pang to see first-hand how much her mother seemed to love her new job, the job that had wrecked everything. Curled up in one of the bookstore's cozy armchairs, Nixie watched her mother's face light up as she recommended a book to a customer whose little boy was fussing. The boy hugged the book and wouldn't let his mom put it down, even when it was time for her to pay.

But if Nixie didn't do the Newer and Even More Improved Plan, she might lose Grace forever.

seven

IN camp on Monday Chef Michael announced that this was bake-sale week. Monday would be cookie-dough-making day. Tuesday would be cookie-baking day. Wednesday they'd decorate whatever cookies needed decorating and start baking the cakes. The rest of the cake-baking and cake-frosting would happen on Thursday. Then they'd sell the cookies and slices of cake in a huge fund-raiser on Friday. The principal was going to advertise the bake sale to the whole school in her *News You Can Use* weekly email home.

First, the campers got to vote for their favorite charity. The choices on the list were the community food pantry, the local art museum, and the Humane Society. Nixie was glad when the Humane Society won. Even if her parents wouldn't let her adopt a dog, at least she could help raise money for dogs that would be adopted by other people.

Or she *would* have helped raise money for dogs if today wasn't going to be her last day at camp ever. Today was the day Nixie had to make herself carry out her Newer and Even More Improved Plan, which also happened to be the scariest Plan yet. But if the Plan worked, Nixie wouldn't be there to bake and decorate any cookies. And Vera, Nolan, and Boogie would have to bake every cake all by themselves.

Every time Nixie thought about the Plan, she felt like an elephant had wrapped his trunk around her chest and was squeezing too tight. But every day she waited would be one more day for Grace and Elyse to get that much closer to being the best friends that Grace and Nixie were supposed to be.

She practiced her speech in her head, imagining how she would make her voice come out sounding weak and trembly. As weak and trembly as she was starting to feel at the thought of actually saying it.

My stomach hurts. I think I'm going to throw up. I need to go home.

Then her mother would have to leave work to come to get her, and she'd see what a bad idea it was to have a job away from home so that her poor daughter had to be sick at camp with no parent to give her loving care. Her mom would gather Nixie into a big comforting hug, settle her on the couch with a fluffy blanket, and read her favorite Betsy-Tacy books aloud to her. And then she would remember that her old work-at-home job had been perfect, after all.

But Nixie didn't have to do the Plan right this minute. She could still have the fun of cookie-dough-making first.

The campers were going to be making dough for chocolate chip cookies, oatmeal raisin cookies, gingersnaps, and butter cookies. Both chefs told the campers not to eat any raw cookie dough: raw dough contained raw eggs, and raw eggs could give you salmonella poisoning.

Boogie ate some chocolate chip cookie dough anyway. And then he ate some of the dough for the oatmeal raisin cookies. At this rate, Nixie thought, Boogie would be the one going up to Colleen with a speech about how his stomach hurt and he was going to throw up and needed to go home.

Nixie wanted so badly to stay to make the gingersnap dough, and the butter cookie dough, and to see if Boogie ate both of those, too. But if she did, by then it would be time for her to go home anyway, sick or not sick, and that wasn't the Plan.

Nixie made herself walk up to where Colleen was helping another team measure out molasses for the gingersnaps.

"My-stomach-hurts-I-think-I'm-going-to-throw-up-I-need-to-go-home," she said, getting the words out as quickly as she could.

"What?" Colleen asked her. "Tell me again, please, *slowly*."

This time Nixie added in some gestures. Hunching her shoulders to look extra-pitiful, she clutched her tummy with both hands and repeated her speech.

Colleen cocked a suspicious eyebrow.

Nixie added her best attempt at gagging,

even though she knew it looked totally fake. But apparently Colleen wasn't in the mood for finding out whether one of her campers was really about to throw up all over the cafeteria floor or just pretending.

The next thing Nixie knew, she was sitting alone in a corner of the cafeteria, holding the bowl Colleen had given her to throw up in.

At least when her mother came, she'd see how pitiful, lonely, and miserable Nixie looked, and her heart would break with guilt over abandoning her own sick daughter to go sell books to other people's healthy kids instead. Tomorrow afternoon Nixie and Grace would be back at Nixie's house again, making their own cookie dough together.

But it wasn't her mom who came walking into the cafeteria ten minutes later.

It was her dad.

☆ ☆ ☆

It was one thing to make fake gagging noises for Colleen; it was another thing to fool her father. Nixie felt her face flaming with guilt at her lie.

"What's going on?" he asked her mildly. "Colleen said you were feeling sick to your stomach? You look fine to me, honey."

"I do feel sick!" It was almost true. The rest came out in a torrent of words: "And I miss Mom, and I want to be with Grace after school again, and I want things to be the way they used to be!"

"Oh, Nixie," was all her father said as he signed her out of camp. But on the car ride home he had seven more things to say, in a no-nonsense voice that drummed each one into Nixie's head:

Nixie's mother loved her job.

Nixie's mother wasn't going to quit her job.

Nixie's father wasn't going to quit his job, either.

Saying you were sick when you weren't sick was lying.

And it was inconsiderate.

And it made people Very Annoyed.

And Nixie should never ever do it again.

After her mother returned from the book-store, she pulled Nixie into a hug that made Nixie feel guiltier still.

"This is a big change for everyone, honey," she said, dropping a kiss on top of Nixie's head, as Nixie snuggled against her. "But change can be a good thing."

Wrong, wrong, wrong, wrong, WRONG.

☆ ☆ ☆

To bake the chocolate chip and oatmeal raisin cookies on Tuesday, Nixie's team dropped the dough in rounded spoonfuls onto lightly greased baking sheets. For the gingersnaps, they made the dough into little balls rolled in granulated sugar, with Nolan making ten balls for every one Vera made. Most fun was rolling out the dough for the butter cookies and then cutting them into various shapes with cookie cutters, as they had with the pet treats.

"So you're feeling better?" Vera asked Nixie as she pressed a perfectly positioned star-shaped cookie cutter into her evenly flattened dough.

It took Nixie a few seconds to figure out what Vera was talking about. Then she felt her cheeks flush. "Uh-huh."

"Did you puke?" Boogie asked hopefully.

"Boogie!" Vera scolded him.

"Well, did you?" Boogie persisted.

Nixie just shook her head.

"I thought maybe you wouldn't be at school today," Vera said.

"Well, I am," Nixie snapped. Why was Vera making her say something so completely obvious? Was Nixie supposed to admit she had been lying yesterday? Yet Nixie couldn't help being glad she was still there at cooking camp. She hated to think of Vera, Nolan, and Boogie baking the cookies without her.

Nolan glanced up from cutting out a series of circle-shaped cookies and gave her a searching look.

He knows, thought Nixie.

☆ ☆ ☆

On Wednesday Chef Maggie showed the campers how to fill plastic baggies with a rainbow of colored icings. Then she showed them how to cut off one tip of the baggie so the icing would come out in a thin, even line.

Nixie's team was decorating "emoticon" cookies: round cookies covered first with bright yellow icing, with eyes and mouths added afterward. If you made the mouth a little round O, the cookie looked surprised. If you added slanted eyebrows, the cookie looked worried. If you put a small red circle on each cheek, the cookie looked embarrassed.

Right now Vera's eyebrows were scrunched like a *very* worried emoticon cookie. She had already cut the smallest possible tip off her baggie to make the narrowest possible icing line. But her icing line was *too* skinny, and when she tried to go over it again to make the mouth thicker, the cookie lips smeared.

"My cookie looks horrible!" Vera practically wailed. "Like—like—a cookie *clown*!"

The cookie looked fine to Nixie. Half of her own cookie smiles and frowns were crooked. So what? The cookies would taste just as yummy with twisty mouths.

Nolan's cookies looked the best so far. He had made a cookie assembly line, as if he was working in a cookie-decorating factory. First, he laid ten cookies in a row on his paper towel and spread them evenly with yellow frosting.

Then he gave all ten cookies two black dots for cookie eyes. Finally, five cookies got smiles, and five cookies got frowns.

"Did you know someone *invented* the smiley face, as a thing?" Nolan asked. "In the 1960s. This guy just sat down and drew a yellow circle and put a smiley face on it, and then everyone in the world started to do it, too."

Boogie had more icing on his hands, arms, face, and T-shirt than on his cookies. Nixie had already seen him eat three cookies, too. If some Humane Society dog somewhere didn't get a new home, it would be Boogie's fault for eating up their fund-raising efforts. She wondered if Boogie's dog had gotten any of their dog biscuits or if Boogie had eaten the whole bag himself.

"Here!" Vera thrust her smudgy cookie at Boogie. "Eat this one!"

Nixie grabbed Boogie's arm to save Vera's cookie in the nick of time.

"We aren't going to have *any* cookies to sell if Vera takes forever to decorate *one* cookie, and then Boogie *eats* it," Nixie protested.

Vera's mouth drooped like a sad-emoticon cookie.

Nixie hadn't meant to make her feel even worse. "I like your cookie," she said. "I would buy it at the bake sale. I would."

"My mother wouldn't," Vera said. "And she's going to come to the bake sale on Friday."

At least Vera's mother would be at the bake sale, unlike Nixie's parents who would be working.

But wait: Why wouldn't Vera's mother be at work, too?

"Won't she be at her job?" Nixie asked.

Vera shook her head. "She takes time off whenever there's something special I'm doing."

"I wouldn't call a bake sale *special*." Nixie inspected her twisty-mouthed cookies, Boogie's cookies that had most of their icing on Boogie, and Vera's cookie with its puffy clown lips. "Not with *these* cookies!"

Vera's eyes crinkled. Was she going to turn into the emoticon cookie that had blue-icing droplets dripping out of its black-dot eyes?

Instead Vera burst out laughing. Relieved, Nixie burst out laughing, too.

"You're funny, Nixie," Vera said, as she squeezed out two perfectly spaced eye dots on her next cookie.

"You're funny, too," Nixie told her. Well, maybe Vera didn't exactly mean to be funny, but sometimes the things she said made Nixie laugh almost as much as she used to do with Grace.

Vera hesitated before making the cookie mouth. Then in a rush she said, "Do you want to come over to my house? Like, this weekend? I want to make a comic book, about animals. You could help me think of funny stuff to put in it."

Nixie felt her cheeks flushing to match the embarrassed-emoticon cookie. She was glad she and Vera were on the same cooking team, and making an animal book sounded like tons of fun. But Nixie couldn't betray Grace that way, she just couldn't. Even if Grace hadn't been following the best-friend rules, Nixie was going to follow them anyway. Otherwise, it would be like saying she and Grace weren't best friends anymore and would never be best friends again.

"I can't," Nixie said. "On the weekends I do stuff with Grace. Because she's, you know, my best friend."

"Oh," Vera said. "That's all right. I understand."

But Vera gave her perfectly iced cookie a perfect little cookie frown.

★ eight ★

THE Longwood Elementary School cafeteria was mobbed after school on Friday for the bake sale. Hungry students and their parents streamed in past tables bearing cookies galore, as well as plastic-wrapped slices of half a dozen different kinds of cake.

Nixie's team stood behind two tables covered with emoticon cookies and delectable slices of German chocolate cake topped with pecan-and-coconut frosting.

"What adorable cookies!" said someone's mother, taking a dozen of the emoticons.

"See?" Nixie said to Vera. "Our cookies do look great!"

Vera gave a small smile. Was she still hurt that Nixie had turned down her invitation for the weekend? Nixie pushed that thought aside.

A group of fifth-graders grabbed five pieces of German chocolate cake. They didn't look interested when Nolan told them that, contrary to its name, German chocolate cake hadn't been invented in Germany. Boogie sighed heavily. "What if the whole entire cake gets bought, and we don't get *any*?"

"Well, you can bake your own German chocolate cake at home," Nixie told him. "Now that you know how."

Vera stood up straighter and smiled more broadly as a tall woman in a peach-colored suit approached their tables.

"I'm sorry I'm late, honey," she told Vera. "I got tied up in a meeting."

"That's okay," Vera said.

"That cake looks scrumptious!" her mother said. "I'll get two slices, one for each of us, and two of the smiley-face cookies. Which ones did you decorate, sweetie? Let me guess." Vera's mother gazed down at the table, her eyes passing over Boogie's smeary faces, which were sure to be the last ones sold, and Nixie's with eyes spaced too widely apart.

"These?" She pointed at two particularly neatly iced cookies. "Am I right?"

"I don't know," Vera said. "It's not like we *signed* our cookies, or anything. We *all* made *all* of them."

"Well, these two look very nice," her mother persisted. "Why don't you introduce me to your friends?"

"Mother, I'd like you to meet Nixie, Nolan, and Boogie," Vera said, as if reciting an approved script of introduction. "Nixie, Nolan, and Boogie, I'd like you to meet my mother, Mrs. Vance."

Her mother gave everyone a gracious smile. "What is your real name?" she asked Boogie.

"Brewster," Boogie muttered.

"What a lovely name! It's a pleasure to meet you, Nixie, Nolan, and Brewster. All right, dear, I'll run back to the office to finish up a few things and come pick you up when camp is over."

"Brewster?" Nolan asked when Vera's mom had left to line up at the payment table where Colleen was taking the money, assisted by a volunteer from the Humane Society. "I didn't know your name was Brewster. Why does everyone call you Boogie?"

"When I was little, I loved to dance, you know, to boogie," Boogie said. "It's not because of boogers!"

Nixie started to laugh, but the laugh died in her throat.

Grace and Elyse were there at her table, followed by a man who had to be Elyse's stay-at-home dad.

"Hi, Nixie!" Elyse was the first to greet her, as if *she* was Nixie's friend as much as Grace.

"Hi, Nixie!" Grace said. "You guys totally have the cutest cookies and the yummiest-looking cake!"

Nixie let herself return Grace's smile. That was exactly what a best friend would say. Best friends were supposed to think everything the other person did was the best.

"They're almost as cute as our puppy cupcakes," Nixie agreed. It didn't hurt to give Grace a reminder of the fun the two of them had shared before Nixie's mother's bombshell had ruined their lives three long weeks ago.

"Let's get smiley-face cookies *and* some cake," Elyse said. "Dad? Can Grace and I get both? Extra snacks because we'll need extra energy to stay up extra-late at our sleepover?"

No.

This couldn't be happening.

But when Nixie stole a glance at Grace, Grace's cheeks were flushed and she was staring very hard in the opposite direction.

How could Grace do this to Nixie? She wouldn't, she couldn't.

Nixie stood absolutely still, shock frozen on her face, like an emoticon Popsicle—arms, legs, mouth encased in a block of ice that would never ever thaw.

Then Grace and Elyse headed off to select more sleepover snacks at other tables.

Suddenly Nixie unfroze, the rage inside her hot enough to shatter the ice and send shards of it flying across the room.

She dashed over to where Grace and Elyse were admiring another team's alphabet-shaped cookies and double-fudge cake.

"Your mother doesn't believe in sleepovers!" she accused Grace.

Grace avoided meeting Nixie's eyes. "We wore her down," was all Grace said.

We wore her down?

How had Grace and Elyse turned into *we*? Why hadn't Grace ever worn her mother down with *Nixie*?

Nixie hurled the next words at Grace: "The only reason you go to Elyse's house is because your parents are too poor to send you to after-school camp with everybody else! Her family felt *sorry* for you!"

It was the worst thing Nixie had ever said to anyone.

And she had said it to her best friend.

Her *former* best friend.

Grace's face crumpled.

"That's not true!" Elyse glared at Nixie and wrapped a protective arm around Grace's shoulders.

The way a true best friend would do.

Nixie wanted to run away from the bake sale, to run away from cooking camp, to run as fast and as far as she could go. But if she ran away, Colleen would call her father again, and her parents would be even madder than when she had lied about being sick.

Slowly she walked back to the bake sale table, where Vera, Nolan, and Boogie stood gaping at her, apparently wondering what was so urgent for her to tell Grace that she had raced off, abandoning them.

"Is everything okay?" Vera asked.

"Of course!" Nixie said brightly. "Everything is completely wonderful."

But she knew it wasn't only Nolan this time, but all three of them, who knew she was lying.

★ nine ★

THUNDERSTORMS canceled the soccer game on Saturday morning. At least Nixie wouldn't have to see Grace and try to figure out what to say to make up for what she had said yesterday. Had Grace told her parents? Would they call Nixie's parents? Nixie knew both sets of parents believed in letting kids work out their quarrels without adult interference. But this was bigger than one little squabble. This was the end of everything.

"I have an idea," her dad said, as rivulets of rain streamed down the kitchen windows. "How about I take you and Grace bowling?"

For a moment Nixie let herself have a tingle of hope. Grace loved bowling. But then she remembered the stricken look on Grace's face at the bake sale.

"Grace doesn't want to be my friend anymore," Nixie said, as if she was reporting one more fact from a long list of true statements: *It's raining today. Soccer is canceled. Grace has a new best friend now.*

"Really?" her dad asked, sounding skeptical. "What happened?"

"What happened is that *Mom* got her new job, and *I* had to go to cooking camp, and *Grace* goes to Elyse's house now, and *Elyse* has a kitten, and *my* parents won't let me have a dog. That's what happened."

Even as she said it, she knew there was one huge, hideous, horrible thing left off the list.

And I said something so mean to Grace that she's never going to forgive me, ever.

Her dad raised an eyebrow. "You and Grace have been good friends for a long time," he finally said. "I don't think a friendship like that ends because of somebody else's kitten. Let's give her a call and see if she's up for knocking down some bowling pins on a rainy morning. What do you say?"

If Nixie said anything more, she'd start to cry. So she scrunched her eyes shut, pressed her lips together, and shook her head back and forth. *No. No. No. No. No!*

"Okay," was all her father said.

But nothing in Nixie's life was ever going to be okay again.

☆ ☆ ☆

On Monday morning Grace didn't exchange a single glance with Nixie during math or spelling or stand in her usual spot next to Nixie during yoga stretches in P.E. She acted as if a person named Nixie Ness didn't even exist.

At lunch Nixie couldn't make herself carry her lunch to Grace and Elyse's table, formerly known as Grace and Nixie's table. She stood uncertainly clutching her purple-pansy lunch bag, looking around for somewhere to sit instead.

Across the room, Vera waved to her.

As Nixie slipped into place beside Vera, she was grateful Vera didn't say, *I thought you always ate with Grace*, so Nixie didn't have to say, *That was then. This is now*.

She listened as Vera talked about how sad she was that this was the final week of cooking camp, but how excited she was that they were going to be cooking the stupendous foods for their grand finale Trip Around the World.

"It sounds like fun," Nixie agreed, to be polite.

But nothing could be fun when your best friend was gone, and it was your fault, and there was no way you could ever make it right again.

☆ ☆ ☆

Chef Michael explained the plans for Trip Around the World Week. Monday: Italy! Tuesday: Mexico! Wednesday: West Africa! Thursday: India! Friday would be the gala Trip Around the World Feast. Campers would get two guest tickets each to invite family members or friends.

"My mom's going to come," Vera told her teammates once Chef Michael had finished talking. "But I sort of wish she wouldn't."

"Why?" Nolan asked.

"Oh, I don't know. It's just that she'll want to know exactly which foods I made, and she'll want them to be better than everybody else's foods. And she'll call Boogie Brewster."

"That's okay," Boogie reassured her. "My

mom calls me Brewster sometimes. Well, only when she's mad. Well, I guess that's pretty often. Anyway, my mom'll want to come, too, but I have three little brothers who'd have to come with her, so I guess she can't."

"Why don't you go home after school if your mom's there with your brothers?" Nixie asked.

"I used to, but my mom said I could do the camp stuff this year because it sounded like such a blast." He lowered his voice: "Plus, I think she wants me to burn up some energy, if you know what I mean."

Nixie and Vera exchanged a grin.

"You can have my extra ticket," Vera told Boogie. "I just need one for my mom."

"You can have one of mine, too," Nolan offered. "I don't need any. My parents can't ever take off from work, and my big sisters are busy with their own stuff."

Nixie took a deep breath, then the words came tumbling out. "I would have invited Grace, because she used to be my best friend, but now she's not, so I have no one to invite, either."

There. She had said it out loud to her whole cooking camp team. She wondered what they'd say, or if they'd say anything at all.

"You could invite her anyway," Vera said slowly. "Just in case."

Nixie shook her head. "She only likes Elyse now."

"Invite Elyse, too!" Boogie suggested. "Everyone likes free food!"

This time Nixie gave another eye-scrunching, lip-pressing head shake. "You don't understand. I said something terrible to Grace. Like, really terrible. Really, really terrible."

"Have you told Grace you're sorry?" Nolan asked.

Nixie stared at him. How could someone who was so brainy and brilliant, who knew so many facts about everything, ask something so dumb, dumb, dumb? She could tell Grace a million times that she was sorry, in a million different ways, but it wouldn't change a thing.

She didn't have to answer Nolan, though, because Colleen swung by their station and handed them two feast tickets apiece, except to Nolan, who only wanted one to give to Boogie.

Nixie wanted to rip her tickets into tiny confetti pieces and toss the whole handful at Vera, Boogie, and Nolan so they'd stop looking at her with their sympathetic, worried eyes. But instead she shoved the tickets into her back jeans pocket, not caring if they got bent.

She'd go ahead and take their advice so they'd see exactly how useless and pointless it was.

She'd invite Grace to the Trip Around the World Feast. Not that she'd come.

She'd invite Elyse, too. Not that Elyse would come, either.

She'd apologize to Grace. Not that it would make any difference.

Or—maybe—maybe—it would?

What if Nixie made Grace the best, yummiest, cooking camp apology ever?

★ ten ★

IT was Thursday, India day, and Nixie's team was making *saag aloo*, which Nixie had never heard of until that afternoon. She hadn't even known what the two words meant. *Saag*? *Aloo*? Nor had she ever tasted any of the spices used to make it: garam masala, turmeric, cumin seeds.

But now she knew: *saag* was spinach, *aloo* was potato, and the spices, when she sniffed them, smelled delicious.

Nolan had heard of *saag aloo*, of course, not only because Nolan had heard of everything, but also because his parents were from India, and his grandparents still lived there, in Delhi.

"*Saag paneer* is spinach with cheese," he told the others. "*Saag gosht* is spinach with goat or any kind of meat."

"Spinach with *goat*?" Boogie asked.

Nixie hoped he wasn't going to say *Yuck!* She could tell Nolan wanted them to like India day. And she did.

She had liked every day of the Trip Around the World. Vera had chopped the garlic and onions for Monday's lasagna with surprising speed. Boogie had kept his fingers out of Tuesday's enchilada filling. Nolan had shared extra-fascinating facts about Nigeria and Ghana as they made African nut stew and *jollof* rice (rice with all kinds of yummy things in it like onions, green peppers, and ginger) on Wednesday.

But Nixie couldn't love Trip Around the World Week with her whole heart because she hadn't apologized to Grace yet. She kept waiting for the special alphabet-letter cookie cutters to arrive by express mail.

Please, please, please, please, let the cookie cutters come today!

The whole Apology Plan depended on them, and Nixie didn't have a Plan B. Actually, this new Plan was really Plan D, her fourth and final Get Your Best Friend Back Plan. Plans

A through C—making Grace a healthy lunch, starring in an online video, and pretending to be sick—had all failed. If the apology failed, too, Nixie was out of Plans completely.

Please, please, please, please, let this Plan work!

The Trip Around the World Feast was tomorrow.

"India has over a billion people," Nolan said, as he stirred the spinach they were "wilting" in a big pot on the stove. Nixie would never have guessed how much a huge box of fresh spinach shrunk down when it was cooked for just a minute or two. "Guess how many languages are spoken there?"

"Ten!" Boogie shouted.

"Fifty?" Vera guessed.

"Well, it depends on what counts as a language, and the number keeps changing, but it's *hundreds*," Nolan told them.

"Wow!" Nixie said.

It was exciting to add the unfamiliar spices to the simmering onions, garlic, ginger, and tomato, to be making food from such an amazing country, on the other side of the world, where a billion people talked to each other in hundreds of different ways.

But right now Nixie just needed to say *I'm sorry* to one person in the only language she knew.

☆ ☆ ☆

The instant her father pulled the car into the garage, Nixie leaped out and ran to the mailbox. The cookie-cutter package was there!

"I have to bake some cookies," Nixie told him. "I have to bake them now. Like, right now. Before we make dinner. Before we do anything." She and her dad could eat whenever they wanted to; her mother was working at the bookstore until it closed at nine.

"Whatever you say, Nix," her dad said good-naturedly.

She hadn't told her parents exactly why she needed the cookie cutters, but she knew they knew it had to do with whatever had happened with Grace.

Nixie had prepared the cookie dough earlier in the week and chilled it in the refrigerator. Now she sprinkled flour on a long piece of waxed paper spread out on the kitchen table. With a floured rolling pin, she flattened the dough to an even thinness. She had already figured out the message she was going to make with the cookies. The recipe was supposed to make four dozen cookies—forty-eight—and she cut carefully to squeeze out one letter more.

The cookies looked beautiful once she had frosted them in stripes and polka dots of five different colors, even though the F in FRIEND broke and she had to use extra frosting to stick it back together. She found a box in the garage, lined the bottom with foil, and spread out the letters:

I AM SORRY
FOR THE MEAN THING I SAID
PLEASE BE MY FRIEND AGAIN

Then she took the cat cookies she had baked yesterday for Cha-Cha (star-shaped because she didn't have any fish-shaped cookie cutters) and layered them in a shoe box covered with pictures of cats cut out from magazines. She slipped the two Trip Around the World Feast tickets into an envelope decorated with hearts and flowers and taped it onto the side of the alphabet-cookie box.

It was the best she could do.

"Can you drive me to Grace's?" Nixie asked, once she had gobbled down her father's chicken stir-fry which didn't taste anywhere near as good as their *saag aloo*.

"Sure," her father said. As Nixie carried the boxes to the car, balancing the cat-cookie box carefully on top of the apology box so as not to jostle a single frosted letter, he added, "I'm proud of you, honey."

"For what?" She hadn't done much to make anybody proud of her lately.

"For trying to fix things with Grace and make them right again."

At Grace's house, Nixie wanted to set the cookies on the doorstep, ring the bell, and race back to the car. But she couldn't do that with her father sitting at the wheel watching her. He'd hardly be proud of her then.

Her heart thumped inside her chest like a hollow drum as Grace's mother opened the door.

"Why, Nixie," Grace's mom said, her voice rising with surprise.

Surely Grace had told her mother the terrible thing Nixie had said. Did Grace's mother hate Nixie now, too?

"I baked these for Grace," Nixie blurted out. "Elyse can have some, too. Everyone can have some. And I baked cookies for Cha-Cha, but nobody else should eat any because they have tuna fish in them, and who, except for a cat, would want to eat fishy cookies? And the envelope has two tickets for the big cooking camp feast tomorrow. And I hope Grace and Elyse can come."

And I hope, I hope, I hope, I hope Grace will be my friend again.

"Don't let the letters get messed up!" Nixie told Grace's mother. "Okay? Keep the box really level. Okay?"

"I'll do my best," Grace's mother said. She opened her mouth to say something else, but Nixie couldn't bear to hear it.

She thrust the boxes at Grace's mother and, swallowing back tears, fled to the car.

Grace wasn't at school on Friday.

Nixie's heart twisted like a wrung-out dish-rag. Had there been something wrong with the cookies? Had her eggs, even baked, been the bad kind that gave people salmonella poison-ing? Maybe Grace was sick, dying, even dead, and Nixie would be a murderer, and no one would believe she hadn't done it on purpose, and she'd go to prison for life.

Plan D would be the hugest failure of all: *D* for a *devastating, distressing, depressing di-saster*.

Maybe she should ask Elyse if she knew why Grace wasn't at school. But Nixie could just imagine Elyse snapping that she wasn't going to answer questions for anybody who could say something as mean as what Nixie had said to Grace on the bake sale day.

"Are you okay?" Vera asked Nixie at lunch. "You look kind of—I don't know—jumpy."

Vera would be jumpy, too, if she was about to be arrested for giving someone salmonella poisoning.

"I'm worried about Grace," Nixie confessed. "I baked some cookies for her—to apologize, the way Nolan said to do—and I took them to her house yesterday, and now she's not at school. What if my cookies made her sick?"

"Your cookies wouldn't make Grace sick," Vera reassured her. "Not unless she got a stomachache from eating *all* of them, and nobody would do a piggish thing like that except for—"

"Boogie." Nixie finished the sentence for her. Even though she might be going to jail for life for poisoning her former best friend, Nixie found herself giggling, and Vera giggled, too.

"Maybe . . ." Nixie said slowly. "This weekend? Would you like to come over? I bet my dad would take us bowling."

Vera's face lit up. "I love bowling! Well, I've never been bowling. But I know I *would* love it!"

"I think you'd love it, too," Nixie said.

She and Vera were more different from each other than she and Grace had ever been, but opposites *could* attract. And she and Grace were more different from each other now than they used to be, but maybe, just maybe, they could be friends again.

★ eleven ★

AFTER school the cafeteria was almost as crowded as it had been for the bake sale. Chefs Maggie and Michael had draped the long tables with colorful tablecloths and covered three of the four cafeteria walls with travel posters: the Leaning Tower of Pisa, the Aztec pyramids, African beaches dotted with thatched-roof bungalows, and the Taj Mahal. The international foods the campers had made all week were ready in warming pans over low heat to be served cafeteria-style. And Nixie and Vera, Boogie and Nolan, and the other cooking campers had made every bite of it.

Boogie's mother turned out to be a round, comfortable-looking woman with big, untidy hair, and a big, toothy smile. His three little brothers were miniature Boogies, racing from table to table, as their mother kept calling after them, "Walk! Don't run!" and "Don't touch any of the food! Nothing at all! I mean it!" Nixie and Vera grinned at each other.

Wearing a plum-colored suit this time, Vera's mother joined them at their table.

"Nixie, Nolan, Brewster, how lovely to see you again," she greeted them.

"It's Boogie, Mother," Vera corrected. "He likes to be called Boogie."

"Well, it's nice to see the three of you," Mrs. Vance said, with a special smile at Boogie, despite his unfortunate choice of name. "And the food you've made looks divine!"

Nixie tried not to mind that Grace and Elyse weren't there. If Grace was sick, she was sick, and Vera was probably right that Nixie's cookies weren't to blame. Or maybe Grace wasn't sick, but she hadn't felt like coming. Or maybe she and Elyse were busy getting ready for another sleepover Nixie wasn't going to be a part of.

Then she saw them, dropped off by Grace's mom, who for some reason wasn't at work. And Grace was on crutches!

"They did come!" Nixie exclaimed.

"See?" Vera gave Nixie a quick hug.

"Everyone likes free food!" Boogie added.

Nolan flashed Nixie a thumbs-up and a big smile.

Slowly Nixie rose from the table and walked over to greet Grace and Elyse.

"I tripped over Cha-Cha yesterday!" Grace told her. "And I hurt my ankle! And my mother thought it might feel better this morning, but it felt even worse, and so she had to take a personal day off from work so I could go to the doctor, and they had to take X-rays, and it took forever, and it's not broken, just sprained, but my mother said I should stay home from school and give it a full day of rest, but I begged and begged to come to your feast, and then she said it was okay. But somebody else has to carry my tray for me!"

"I will!" Nixie said, just as Elyse said, "I will!"

"You both can," Grace said, giving each of them a huge grin. "You can take turns."

Long lines were starting to form for the food now. As Elyse dashed off to grab a tray for Grace, Nixie held back.

"I really am sorry," she whispered to Grace. It wasn't enough to say it in cookie language. She wanted to say it in real words, too.

Grace's eyes glistened with tears. "I am, too. I just felt so left out that you were going to After-School Superstars without me. But then Elyse and I made *you* feel left out." She paused. "Do you want to have a sleepover sometime? Just you and me? Now that my mom finally let me?"

Nixie felt herself beaming. "Yes! Just you and me! But then—maybe we could have another one, for you and me and Elyse and Vera, too."

Grace beamed an even bigger smile back at her.

Half an hour later Nixie was as stuffed as stuffed could be, full of lasagna, enchiladas, nut stew and *jollof* rice, and *saag aloo*.

Chef Maggie tapped a spoon on a glass to call the room to silence.

"Let's thank our student chefs for preparing this extraordinary Trip Around the World Feast for us today!" Chef Maggie paused for the applause. "And they've also starred in a

brand-new episode of our *Kids Can Cook* video series, which we'll post online next week. We're going to give you a sneak preview of it right now."

The cafeteria shades came down at the touch of a button and the lights dimmed. Projected on the one blank wall of the cafeteria, the video began with a panoramic sweep over a field of bright orange pumpkins, followed by a close-up of one huge, perfect pumpkin gleaming in the afternoon sunshine.

It was fine that Nixie's team wasn't going to be in the video. She didn't need that Plan anymore.

But a few minutes into the video, after it seemed as if every other group of campers except for Nixie's team had been shown, there Vera was, projected up on the wall.

"Make sure you take the time to do your work carefully," said the voice of the narrator, as a larger-than-life Vera frowned over her perfect chopping. Nixie reached over and squeezed Vera's hand as Vera's mother gave her daughter a nod of approval.

"Precise measuring produces the best results."

A larger-than-life Nolan scooped out an exact teaspoonful of salt.

"But don't steal tastes in between!"

A larger-than-life Boogie popped a piece of pumpkin into his mouth, and the room broke out in gales of laughter.

"That's me!" Boogie shouted proudly. "That's me!"

The only one who hadn't appeared in the video yet was Nixie. That was okay, Nixie told herself. Grace and Vera both liked her anyway. Nolan and Boogie liked her, too. And even Elyse was acting so friendly here at the feast. Actually, until the big fight at the bake sale, Elyse had acted friendly all along.

The video was almost over. The background music swelled ever louder in an end-of-movie way.

Then the last image came onto the wall: Nixie's own larger-than-life face, stirring the pumpkin soup with her big movie-star smile, right before she had stirred so hard she burned her wrist.

Nixie couldn't take her eyes off the girl in the video, who looked so strange, but so familiar, too: a girl with stubby braids who was having a wonderful time at an after-school cooking camp.

Surrounded by friends.

Nixie's Favorite Recipe from Cooking Camp

☆ Morning Glory Muffins ☆

Be sure to get permission and assistance from an adult first.

Ingredients

2 cups whole wheat flour

2 tsp baking soda

2 tsp cinnamon

½ tsp ground ginger

¼ tsp salt

2 cups grated carrot

2 cups grated apple

½ cup coconut flakes

½ cup chopped walnuts

¼ cup sunflower seeds, shelled and unsalted

3 large eggs

2 tsp vanilla extract

¼ cup orange juice

⅓ cup honey

½ cup vegetable oil

½ cup seedless raisins

Directions

Preheat oven to 375 degrees.

Combine dry ingredients in large mixing bowl (flour, baking soda, cinnamon, ginger, salt).

Stir in carrots, apples, coconut flakes, walnuts and sunflower seeds so they are coated with the flour mixture.

In a separate bowl, whisk together eggs, vanilla, orange juice, honey, and oil.

Fold in the raisins.

Spoon into lightly greased muffin pan (the recipe makes 18 muffins).

Bake for around 18 minutes (a bit less for darker pans).

Acknowledgments

I can't express enough thanks to the children's book superstars at Holiday House who helped make Nixie's story as starry as could be. Margaret Ferguson is the editor every author dreams of, offering the perfect blend of encouragement and unfailingly insightful critique. Raina Putter and John Simko offered sharp-eyed corrections I would have otherwise missed. Kerry Martin created a delightful design for the series.

My superstar agent, Stephen Fraser, has cheered me on for book after book; his steadfast support means so much to me. Writer friends read drafts at every stage: heartfelt thanks to the Writing Roosters (Jennifer Bertman, Jennifer Sims, Laura Perdew, Vanessa Appleby, and Tracy Abell) and to Ann Whitehead Nagda, Leslie O'Kane, and Kate Simpson.

Grace Zong's lively pictures bubble over with happy energy. I hug myself with happiness every time I look at them.

A plaintive Facebook query for a simplified *saag* recipe that could be made by ambitious third-graders yielded assistance from brilliant children's author Varsha Bajaj. Yum!

Tanky-the-dog tested the dog biscuits—and the cat cookies, too. Human family members patiently sampled the other results from my test kitchen (the

Morning Glory muffins ended up receiving their highest rating).

Finally, Wina Mortenson, hilarious children's librarian in Galesville, Wisconsin, served as my expert on how to structure an after-school program, offering terrific suggestions that found their way into the finished book. It's a joy to be able to claim her as a friend.

Read on for a sneak peek at more

AFTER-SCHOOL SUPERSTARS FUN!

AFTER-SCHOOL SUPERSTARS
VERA VANCE
COMICS STAR

Claudia Mills ★ pictures by Grace Zong

★ one ★

BAM! BOOM! KAPOW!

Vera Vance let go of her bowling ball, hoping this time to hear ten pins exploding into the air. But her ball rolled so slowly and crookedly down the lane again that only one pin, on the far left, wobbled for a second before toppling over.

"Hooray!" Nixie Ness shouted, pumping her fist.

Vera didn't have a lot of friends yet. She and her mother had moved to Longwood for her mother's new job right before school began two months ago. But she and Nixie had just finished being in an after-school cooking camp together, and now Nixie had invited her to come bowling on Saturday afternoon.

Vera stared at Nixie. "Hooray?"

"You got a point! Your first point!"

"You're starting to figure it out," Nixie's father chimed in, sounding almost as enthusiastic as Nixie herself.

Vera couldn't help laughing. So far the only thing she had figured out in her first time ever bowling was that she was terrible at it. Nixie was almost as bad at bowling as Vera. The difference between Vera and Nixie was that when Nixie knocked down a single pin, she started talking about how she was going to be the third-grade bowling champion of the world. Vera just saw the other nine pins still standing.

"Roll again," Nixie's father told her. "You have another roll coming to you."

This time, to Vera's astonishment, four more pins went down.

"See!" Nixie squealed. "Didn't I tell you you'd be great at bowling?"

Vera felt herself beaming. She could imagine drawing a comic of the bowling pins flying into the air with surprised expressions on their faces. All Vera could think about these days was making comics: on Monday, the After-School Superstars program she and Nixie attended was starting a four-week comic-book camp.

As Nixie readied herself for her next turn, Vera wondered whether the bowling pins should look sad instead of surprised when they got smashed by the bowling ball. It was hard not to feel sorry for the poor bowling pins, standing up straight and proud one moment, then clobbered the next.

No, Vera decided. Right this minute— bowling with Nixie and looking forward to comic-book camp together—she wasn't going to think sad thoughts about anything.

☆ ☆ ☆

The next day, Nixie came over to Vera's house after lunch. They had never had a play-date before, and now they were having two in the same weekend. Once Nixie's family had invited Vera to go bowling, Vera's mother had immediately issued an invitation of their own to Nixie. She called it "reciprocating." Vera knew her mother liked to get "reciprocating" over with as soon as possible.

"What do you want to do?" Vera asked as soon as her mother had welcomed Nixie and then tactfully disappeared into the home office where she did stuff for her job as a financial planner.

"I don't know. What do you want to do?" Nixie replied.

Vera felt a twinge of nervousness. It was easier to go bowling with a friend because then it was obvious what you were supposed to do: bowl! For an at-home playdate you were supposed to play. But what if the other person didn't like playing the same things you did?

"I know!" Nixie said. Vera relaxed. "Show me your room! Didn't you tell me you were making a comic book about animals? I love animals! Well, dogs mainly. Not cats. But if there are cats in your book, that's okay, too."

Half an hour later the girls were lying on Vera's neatly made bed, side by side, drawing dogs. Vera's dogs looked more like dogs than Nixie's did, because Vera borrowed details from her big animal encyclopedia, while Nixie just made them up out of her head. But Nixie was great at thinking of funny things for the dogs to be doing and saying.

"How about they go to a doggie school?"

Nixie suggested. "Like maybe it's called Bow-Wow Elementary."

Vera thought for a moment. "Or Mistress Barker's Bow-Wow Academy."

"Yes! That's perfect!" Nixie shouted. "What street should it be on?"

The answer came to Vera instantly. "Wag-a-Tail Lane."

Nixie tossed a fistful of colored pencils into the air in clear appreciation of Vera's brilliance. The pencils clattered onto the hardwood floor.

Just then Vera's mother poked her head into the room. "It sounds like you two are having fun," she said.

"Are we making too much noise?" Vera asked.

"No, not at all," her mother said. "Well, maybe a tiny bit." She smiled when she said it. Vera knew her mother wanted her to have friends in Longwood as much as she did.

"Vera is a great draw-er," Nixie said.

"Nixie is a terrific artist, too," Vera said in return.

Nixie's face lit up. "If we get to have partners in comic-book camp, let's work together.

Our comic book will totally be the best! We could make a whole Bow-Wow Academy comic, with the dogs as superheroes, each one with a different superpower. Not just superbarking, or superbiting, or super-peeing-on-fire-hydrants, but really cool superpowers, like turning into other animals—like maybe one dog turns into an elephant and can spray water from her trunk to put out fires!"

If they had to have comic-book partners, of course Vera wanted Nixie for hers. But part of Vera hoped they'd get to work alone. What if she and Nixie disagreed on ideas? So far they had agreed on everything about Mistress Barker's Bow-Wow Academy. But in the space of a minute Nixie had already gone ahead and practically planned out the whole book.

Before Vera could think of how to reply to Nixie, her mother said, "I'm not sure Vera's doing the comic-book camp."

No! Not that again! Vera's mother had been talking about hiring a sitter to drive Vera to some other enrichment activity instead, like the kids' Science Discovery class at the university. She always told Vera comics weren't "real literature," but Vera devoured comics and graphic novels in the library at school. She loved everything about them—the way she could be swept along in the story by the words *and* the pictures and feel like she was right there having adventures side by side with kids so much braver than she could ever be.

The camp was starting tomorrow! Her mother couldn't change her mind about it one day before the most wonderful camp in the world was going to begin.

Could she?

Nixie opened her mouth as if she was about to explain to Mrs. Vance how Vera *had* to be in the comic-book camp, she just *had* to. But then Nixie's mouth closed again. It was clear Vera's mother wasn't someone who could be told what she *had* to do.

"I want to go to the comic-book camp," Vera said in a small voice.

"I know you do," her mom replied. "But why would a school *enrichment* program devote an entire camp to *comic* books when there are so many other truly important things in the world to learn about?"

Vera stared down silently at the dog pictures she and Nixie had drawn. If only Nixie hadn't mentioned dogs peeing on fire hydrants! That was exactly the kind of thing her mother didn't like.

Her mother sighed. "Honey, I'm willing to give the comic-book camp a try for now. But if you're bored because it's not challenging enough, we can make whatever changes in your schedule we need to. All right, girls, I'll let you go back to your fun."

Vera's mother gave both girls a smile before heading downstairs again.

After a moment of silence, Nixie said, "She did say you could do the camp."

"She said I could do it *for now*."

"Can you talk to your dad?"

Vera took a deep breath. "I don't have a dad. He died in a car accident when I was two."

Nixie's face crumpled. "I shouldn't have . . . I mean . . . I didn't know. I'm sorry, Vera."

"That's okay." Vera was used to answering questions about her dad in a matter-of-fact voice without making the other person feel bad for having asked. But this time her voice had come out shakier than usual. "Well, let's draw some more."

"I'm tired of drawing."

Vera knew Nixie hadn't been the tiniest bit tired of drawing before her mother had come into the room.

"I have an idea!" Nixie said. "Let's look at animal pictures in your encyclopedia and each pick out the top ten animals we'd adopt if our parents let us have pets."

"Okay," Vera agreed.

But she didn't care if her mother might someday let her have a dog, or an elephant, or a pygmy three-toed sloth. She only cared whether her mother would let her keep going to comic-book camp after school every single day for a whole entire month.

Claudia Mills is the acclaimed author of more than sixty books for children, including the Franklin School Friends series and the middle-grade novel *Zero Tolerance*. She recently received the Kerlan Award. She lives in Boulder, Colorado.

Grace Zong has illustrated many books for children, including *Goldy Luck and the Three Pandas* by Natasha Yim and *Mrs. McBee Leaves Room 3* by Gretchen Brandenburg McLellan. She divides her time between South Korea and New York.